LAND OF YING
TWEEG'S MUM'S
THE GREAT WALL OF YING
M.A.V.O. HEADQUARTERS
LEEKEE LAKE
BEN'S BEACH
RAINBOW FALLS
MIZLEY MEADOWS
MOSS OREST
WOOLY WHAT'S-ITS
WEEG'S WER
GIMMICK'S VALLEY
BOGGLEY WOODS
OODLEY BOG
RILLONIA

One day Teddy Ruxpin and his friends Newton Gimmick and Grubby set off for a quiet picnic in Boggley Woods. But their plans change when they meet Amanda, a ladybird who is trying to win another spot by doing a good deed. Amanda takes Teddy and his friends to the Bug Fair, where fun and surprises await them all.

British Library Cataloguing in Publication Data
Miller, Dennis
Fun at the fair.
I. Title
823'.914[J]
ISBN 0-7214-1168-1

Designed by Gavin Young

First edition

Published by Ladybird Books Ltd Loughborough Leicestershire UK
Ladybird Books Inc Auburn Maine 04210 USA

Printed in England

Fun at the fair

adapted by DENNIS MILLER

Ladybird Books

It was a fine, sunny day in the Land of Grundo. Teddy Ruxpin and his friends Newton Gimmick and Grubby were in the mood for an adventure.

"Why don't we go for a picnic?" suggested Gimmick. Teddy and Grubby agreed that a picnic was a very good idea.

Grubby went to the kitchen to collect the food, while Gimmick found the picnic cloth and basket.

Soon everything was packed on board the Airship.
"Stand by for lift-off," cried Gimmick.
"Full speed on the propeller, Grubby!"

They soared in the air high above Grundo and came in to land at Boggley Woods. It was the perfect spot for a picnic!

Teddy spread the picnic cloth on the grass and they all helped to unpack the food.

Grubby picked up a shiny red apple.

But just as he was about to eat it, he noticed that one of the bowls was moving across the cloth!

The bowl was followed by two bananas, a piece of celery and a tomato. Next, some cheese staggered away, just ahead of a sandwich.

"Our food is disappearing!" cried Grubby. He was very alarmed.

"So it is!" exclaimed Gimmick.

"I wonder why?" said Teddy.

"There could be several scientific reasons..." Gimmick began, but Teddy interrupted him.

"I think it's bugs!" he said.

Teddy was right! Their food was being carried off by an army of little insects!

"They're ladybirds!" said Teddy.

One ladybird, who appeared to be in charge, sang as the others marched in time to her words:

LAND OF YING
TWEEG'S MUM'S
THE GREAT WALL OF YING
M.A.V.O. HEADQUARTERS
LEEKEE LAKE
BEN'S BEACH
RAINBOW FALLS
MIZLEY MEADOWS
OREST
WOOLY WHAT'S-ITS
GIMMICK'S VALLEY
BOGGLEY WOODS
RILLONIA

One day Teddy Ruxpin and his friends Newton Gimmick and Grubby set off for a quiet picnic in Boggley Woods. But their plans change when they meet Amanda, a ladybird who is trying to win another spot by doing a good deed. Amanda takes Teddy and his friends to the Bug Fair, where fun and surprises await them all.

British Library Cataloguing in Publication Data
Miller, Dennis
Fun at the fair.
I. Title
823'.914[J]
ISBN 0-7214-1168-1

Designed by Gavin Young

First edition

Published by Ladybird Books Ltd Loughborough Leicestershire UK
Ladybird Books Inc Auburn Maine 04210 USA

Printed in England

Fun at the fair

adapted by DENNIS MILLER

Ladybird Books

It was a fine, sunny day in the Land of Grundo. Teddy Ruxpin and his friends Newton Gimmick and Grubby were in the mood for an adventure.

“Why don’t we go for a picnic?” suggested Gimmick. Teddy and Grubby agreed that a picnic was a very good idea.

Grubby went to the kitchen to collect the food, while Gimmick found the picnic cloth and basket.

Soon everything was packed on board the Airship.

"Stand by for lift-off," cried Gimmick. "Full speed on the propeller, Grubby!"

They soared in the air high above Grundo and came in to land at Boggley Woods. It was the perfect spot for a picnic!

Teddy spread
the picnic cloth
on the grass
and they all
helped to
unpack the food.

Grubby picked up a shiny red apple.

But just as he was about to eat it,
he noticed that one of the bowls
was moving across the cloth!

The bowl was followed by two bananas, a piece of celery and a tomato. Next, some cheese staggered away, just ahead of a sandwich.

"Our food is disappearing!" cried Grubby. He was very alarmed.

"So it is!" exclaimed Gimmick.

"I wonder why?" said Teddy.

"There could be several scientific reasons…" Gimmick began, but Teddy interrupted him.

"I think it's bugs!" he said.

Teddy was right! Their food was being carried off by an army of little insects!

"They're ladybirds!" said Teddy.

One ladybird, who appeared to be in charge, sang as the others marched in time to her words:

March to the left!
March to the right!

March, you ladybirds,
with all your might!

Teddy spoke to the head ladybird.

"Excuse me, Miss," he said. "Where are you taking our food?"

"What do you mean!" replied the ladybird as she hopped onto Teddy's nose. "This food belongs to us."

When Teddy showed her the picnic basket and explained that they had brought the food for a picnic, the ladybird jumped down. She was very embarrassed.

"I thought the food was just growing here," she said. "I knew it was too good to be true!"

She made her team of ladybirds put the food back.

"Thank you very much," said Teddy. "Miss... Miss...?"

"Amanda," said the ladybird. She gave a deep sigh, and looked sad.

Teddy asked Amanda why she looked unhappy.

"Because I'll never get a new spot now," she replied.

"A new spot?" said Grubby.

"Yes. A new spot on my wings as a reward for doing a good deed. I was sure I'd get one for taking all this food for everyone to share at the Bug Fair."

"What's a Bug Fair?" asked Teddy.

"Well," said Amanda, "once a year, we insects get together and hold a fair. It's lots of fun. There are games and rides and..."

"...Best of all," put in a ladybird with curly blonde hair, "we have the annual Spot Awards for ladybirds who have done good deeds."

Teddy asked Amanda if they could help her to do a good deed, but she shook her head.

"We have to do them all by ourselves," she explained. "But you're very welcome to come with us to the Bug Fair."

Teddy and his friends accepted at once. Then Amanda groaned and said, "But you will be a BIG problem!"

"Us?" exclaimed Grubby in astonishment.

"Yes. You're all so big that you'll scare the other bugs away," said Amanda.

Teddy smiled. "We won't be a problem!" he cried.

Teddy sent Gimmick back to the Airship to fetch their special portable reducing machine.

It looked like an old-fashioned camera on three legs.

Teddy and Grubby stood in front of it as though they were about to have their picture taken. Then Gimmick pressed a button and ran round to join his friends.

The machine made some clicking noises. Then there was a flash and Teddy, Grubby and Gimmick shrank down until they were the same size as the ladybirds!

They could go to the Bug Fair after all!

Amanda made sure that she introduced her new friends to all the insects at the Bug Fair. Then she showed them all the sights.

First they went to see the twig-lifting contest, which was won by Samson Strongbug, who set a new world record. Then they had a ride on the Acorn Coaster, which whizzed them round and round and up and down until they were quite dizzy.

Next it was time for the Bug Circus, held in the Bug Top. Here they saw a tightrope act with the Amazing Weevils, followed by the Daring Young Fleas on the Flying Trapeze.

At last it was time for the Ladybird Spot Awards.

Amanda was very glum as the Bugmaster of Ceremonies picked up a megaphone and got ready for his announcements.

"Never mind, Amanda!" said Teddy. "Even if you don't win a spot, we're still your friends!"

Amanda smiled bravely. "Thank you!" she said. "Maybe I'll win another spot next year."

But she looked very sad as the winning ladybirds went to have their new spots painted on by the artist.

Suddenly there was a fanfare. The Bugmaster cleared his throat for a special announcement!

"Today," said the Bugmaster, "Amanda could easily have spent her time trying to win another spot. Instead, she made sure that her new friends enjoyed themselves.

"As everyone knows, the very best deed that anyone can do is to make new friends and be nice to them. So, because Amanda has made *three* new friends, she has won *three* new spots!"

The audience cheered and clapped as Amanda proudly went up on stage to receive her new spots. Grubby, Teddy and Gimmick beamed with pleasure. They had helped Amanda to win her new spots after all!

All too soon the day came to an end. It was time for Teddy, Gimmick and Grubby to say goodbye to their new friends.

Amanda and the other bugs went back with them to the Airship, where they put the portable reducing machine into reverse and were soon back to their usual size.

"Goodbye!"
shouted Teddy as the Airship took to the skies. "See you again!"

"Yes!" cried Amanda and her friends. "Come back soon!"

HARD TO FIND
BIRD PEOPLE
KING NOGBURT'S CASTLE
WIZARD OF GRUNDO
JUNGLE WITH NO NAME
MUSHROOM FOREST
LEOTA'S SCHOOLHOUSE
TREMBLY FAULT
THE GREAT DESERT
Land of GRUNDO
CAVES